D1479949

Luke the World Traveler

Welcome to America!

REUBEN LAURORE
Illustrations by Blueberry Illustrations

ISBN: 978-0-578-43366-0

I have to start by thanking my incredible wife, Alexandra. From reading early drafts to editing my chicken scratch, she consistently encouraged me to finish what I started when times were rough. She was as important to this book getting done as I was. Thank you so much, you are truly the spine of this book.

Next, I would like to thank our first born son Lucas Gabriel whom inspired me to create Luke the World Traveler. He is a bright young man who will reach unimaginable heights and succeed in all that he does. From the beginning he has always made me proud. I love you son.

Finally, I would like to thank Kevin Anderson & Associates for their editorial work, Blueberry Illustrations for bringing my vision to life, my friends, family and my coworkers at Tesla for all of your support. Thank you everyone for helping my dream come true!

"Breakfast time," Luke's mom called out from the kitchen. Luke ran out of his room, jumped onto the stairwell railing and slid all the way down.

"Good morning!" Luke greeted
his parents with a big smile.
"Good morning, son."
His father replied while his mom
brought breakfast to the table.
"Are you excited for Flag Day at school, Luke?"
His mom asked.
"I am excited. I can't wait to tell my
class about the United States of America."
Luke gobbled down his food and ran upstairs to get
dressed and put on an American flag cape he made.
He headed for the front door, gave his dad a high-
five and shouted, "Let's hit the road, Mom!"

After Luke hugged his mom goodbye, he walked into his classroom and he couldn't believe his eyes. There were flags from all around the world hanging everywhere and the smell of new foods filled the air. Luke was very curious about which flags belonged to each of his friends and he couldn't wait to learn about the different countries their families were from.

The teacher, Miss Julie, stood in front of
the class while everyone took their seats.
"Good morning everyone and welcome to Flag Day!"
She explained that there are many
countries around the world and that it is
important to learn about their customs
and cultures so that we can celebrate
the things that make us all special.

Miss Julie told her class that customs are
traditions that have been passed down
to us from our families and friends.
"Learning about each other will teach us to respect
one another even though we are all different.
We are going to start today off with a very special
country, the United States of America. This is where
we live, and Luke is going to tell us more about it."

Luke stood up, took a deep breath and began.
"My name is Luke and I am a proud American.
America is a country made up of 50 states.
It became free on July 4, 1776.
We call this Independence Day and we celebrate
with our families and lots of fireworks!"

Luke walked over to the map on the wall and
pointed to Washington D.C., the U.S. capital. "This
is where our President lives, in a big white house."

Luke also showed his class pictures of places to visit.
"Some important places to visit in America are
the Grand Canyon, the Lincoln Memorial
and the Statue of Liberty."

He then told them about the people that protect our country like soldiers, police officers and firefighters. Luke explained how they all work together to protect us like real-life superheroes!

Luke went to the radio and started playing music.
"What kind of music is that?"
Maria asked as everyone started dancing.
"Hip-hop! It's one of the most popular kinds of
music in America," He said as he did a cool
dance move. "Some other types of popular
music are pop, country and rock n' roll."

After the song was over, Luke was asked about
the food in America. "My favorite foods to eat are
macaroni and cheese and grilled cheese sandwiches.
I love when my mom makes me a grilled
cheese sandwich with tomato soup for lunch!"

Luke explained that there are also different styles of food from other countries that we eat here like tacos from Mexico or Sushi from Japan. "America is great because different people from all around the world come to live here, bringing their favorite foods and other parts of their culture with them."

Luke stood up tall and said in a loud voice, "I love America because of our freedoms, all of the different people here and because I can be anything I want to be when I grow up!" Luke's class clapped their hands.

After school, Luke went home, washed up and told his mom and dad about his day. They were very proud of him. He finished all of his dinner then brushed his teeth.

Luke couldn't stop thinking about all of the places he had learned about, and how much he wanted to visit them all. Suddenly he came up with a great idea.

Using his imagination, Luke grabbed pillows, blankets and chairs and started building a tent. When it was finished, he took a step back and thought about where he wanted to go first. Luke wanted to visit one of the places he had told his class about in America.

His dad walked by, saw his tent and asked if he could join him. They walked up to the tent, placed the American flag in front, clapped their hands three times and came up with a magic password, "Wham-Bam-Let's-All-Scram!"

The room started shaking and a bright light sparkled from inside of the tent.

Luke and his dad crawled inside and suddenly
they were staring up at the Statue of Liberty.

He followed his dad as they entered the door by
her giant green feet. They walked all the way
up a staircase that went around and around
until they got to the top of her crown.

Luke and his Dad walked past the windows that looked out over the water and could see New York City in the distance. Luke was very excited to be there, since the Statue of Liberty is an important symbol of freedom and friendship.

By the time they got back down to the bottom
it was already late and time to go back home.
They clapped their hands three times
and said "Wham-Bam-Let's-All-Scram!"
They were back in the playroom!

"That was awesome. With the magic tent, my classmates and I can visit their countries, too! Can I have some friends over tomorrow? Please?" Luke wanted to invite all of his friends over to travel to the places they taught him about.

Luke's dad smiled. "Of course you can. Let's get you to bed so you can get some rest and be ready for your big adventure tomorrow."

His dad carried him upstairs, tucked him in and turned the lights off. He kissed him on the head and said, "Goodnight Luke, my world traveler."

The End